For my mum. You always told me "to keep on trying".
At least, that's what I thought you said...

First published 2013 by Walker Books Ltd, 87 Vauxhall Walk, London SE11 5HJ • This edition published 2013
10 9 8 7 6 5 4 3 2 1 • © 2013 Andy Pritchett • The right of Andy Pritchett to be identified as author/illustrate
of this work has been asserted by him in accordance with the Copyright, Designs and Patents Act 1988 • This boo
has been typeset in Imperfect Bold, Cooper Five Opti Black, Countryhouse, Goudy Stout and Kosmic • Printe
in China • All rights reserved. No part of this book may be reproduced, transmitted or stored in an informatic
retrieval system in any form or by any means, graphic, electronic or mechanical, including photocopying, taping an
recording, without prior written permission from the publisher. • British Library Cataloguing in Publication Data:
catalogue record for this book is available from the British Library • ISBN 978-1-4063-4815-6 • www.walker.co.u

# STICK!

**Andy Pritchett**

WALKER BOOKS

AND SUBSIDIARIES

LONDON • BOSTON • SYDNEY • AUCKLAND

Worm!

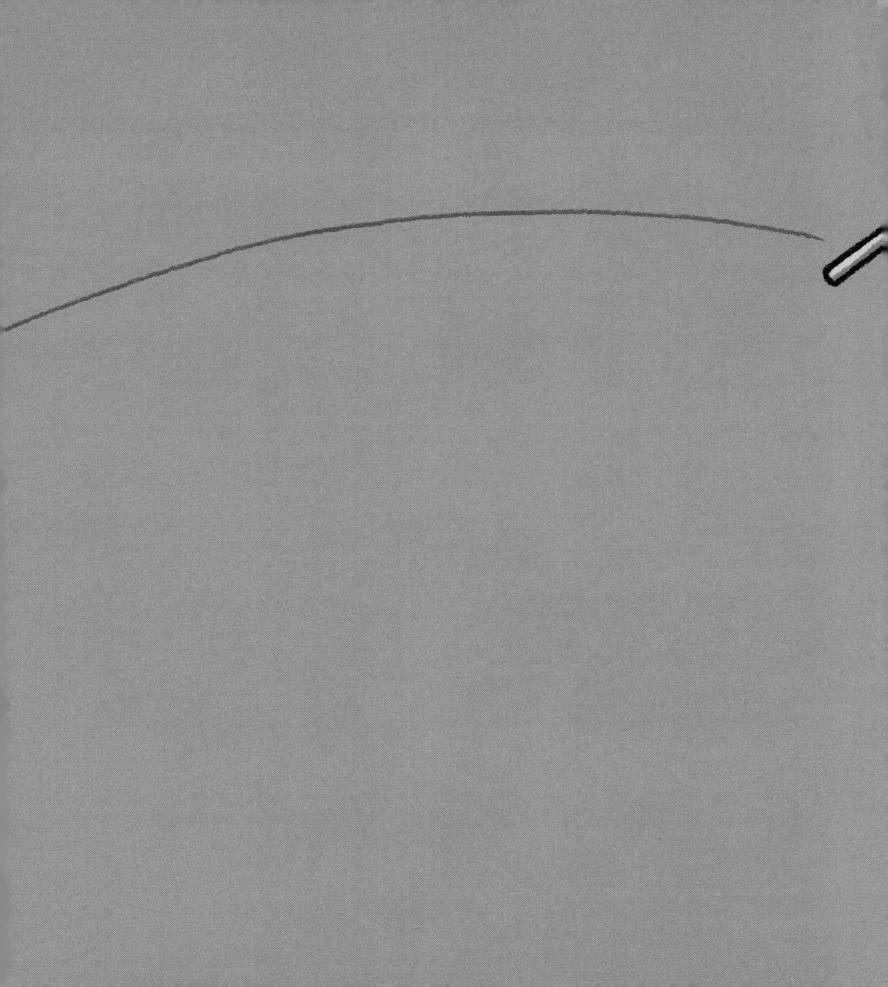

CLUNK!

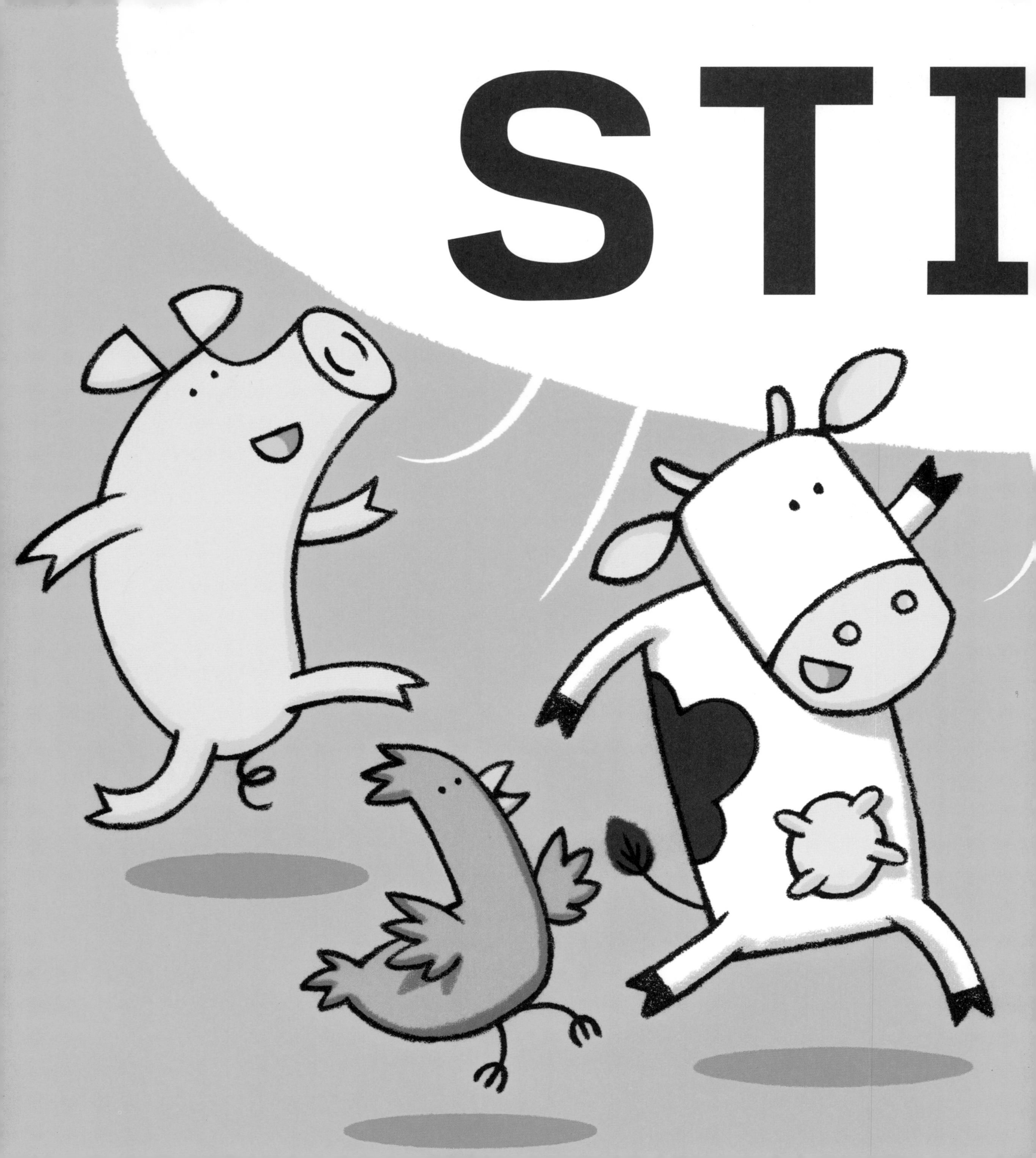
STI

**Friend?**